The Night You Were Born

With love for Brenna and Haley,
two lights, shining, shining — W.R.M.

To Holly and Tess — S.W.

Published by
PEACHTREE PUBLISHERS, LTD.
494 Armour Circle, NE
Atlanta, Georgia 30324

Text © by Wendy McCormick 2000
Illustrations © by Sophy Williams 2000

First published by Orchard Books in Great Britain, 1999

10 9 8 7 6 5 4 3 2 1
First printing

Printed in Singapore

Library of Congress Cataloging-in-Publication Data

McCormick, Wendy
   The night you were born / Wendy McCormick ; illustrated by Sophy Williams.-- 1st ed.
      p. cm.
Summary: As he waits at home with his aunt for his baby sister to be born at the hospital,
a young boy hears what his aunt did while waiting for him to be born.
   ISBN 1-56145-225-4
[1. Babies--Fiction. 2. Brothers and sisters--Fiction. 3. Aunts--Fiction.] I. Sophy, ill. II. Title.
PZ7.M13695 Ni 2000
[E]--dc21

oo-008582

The Night You Were Born

Wendy McCormick

illustrated by Sophy Williams

PEACHTREE

ATLANTA

The night that Jamie's sister was to be born,
Jamie was waiting for her at home,
all night long, all alone.

Well, he wasn't all alone.
Jamie's two cats were there,
sleeping on the windowsill in the kitchen.

Oh, and Jamie's Aunt Isabel was there, too,
washing up soup bowls from their dinner.

"Will Mommy and Daddy remember me,"
Jamie asked her,
"waiting here all night long?"

"Of course they will," Aunt Isabel said.
"You know, waiting is a big job—
an important job."

"We have to light the way for
this new baby," said Aunt Isabel.
So they went to the front hall
and turned on the light over
the front door.

And they went to the back hall
and turned on the light over the back door.

"I waited for you, too, you know,"
Aunt Isabel told him, "the night you were born."
"You did?" asked Jamie
as the two of them started upstairs.

"Yes," Aunt Isabel said.
"But you were so very late," she said.
"We waited and waited."

Aunt Isabel turned on the lights
in Jamie's room.
Jamie switched on his nightlight
shaped like a seashell.

"What did you do while you
waited for me?" he asked as
he made a pile of pillows on his bed.
"That's a long story," Aunt Isabel replied
as they snuggled up with Jamie's two cats.

Jamie flipped on his flashlight and he
shined it on the ceiling. "Where were you?"
he asked.

"The night you were born,
I was far away from here," said Aunt Isabel.
"Your uncle and I were driving here to meet you.
We knew you were on your way, too.
But we weren't sure when you'd arrive."

"That morning had been the foggiest morning we'd ever seen.
'Is this the day?' I wondered.
'The day that he'll be born?'
The fog settled around us,
thick as a nest of furry rabbits."

"Was it the day?" Jamie asked.
Aunt Isabel kissed the top of Jamie's head.
"You'll see," she said.

"We phoned the hospital from the misty road.
'Is today the day?' I asked.
'We don't know yet,' they told me.
'Nothing yet,' I said to your uncle."

"I was very late," Jamie told Aunt Isabel.
"Very," Aunt Isabel said as she began again.

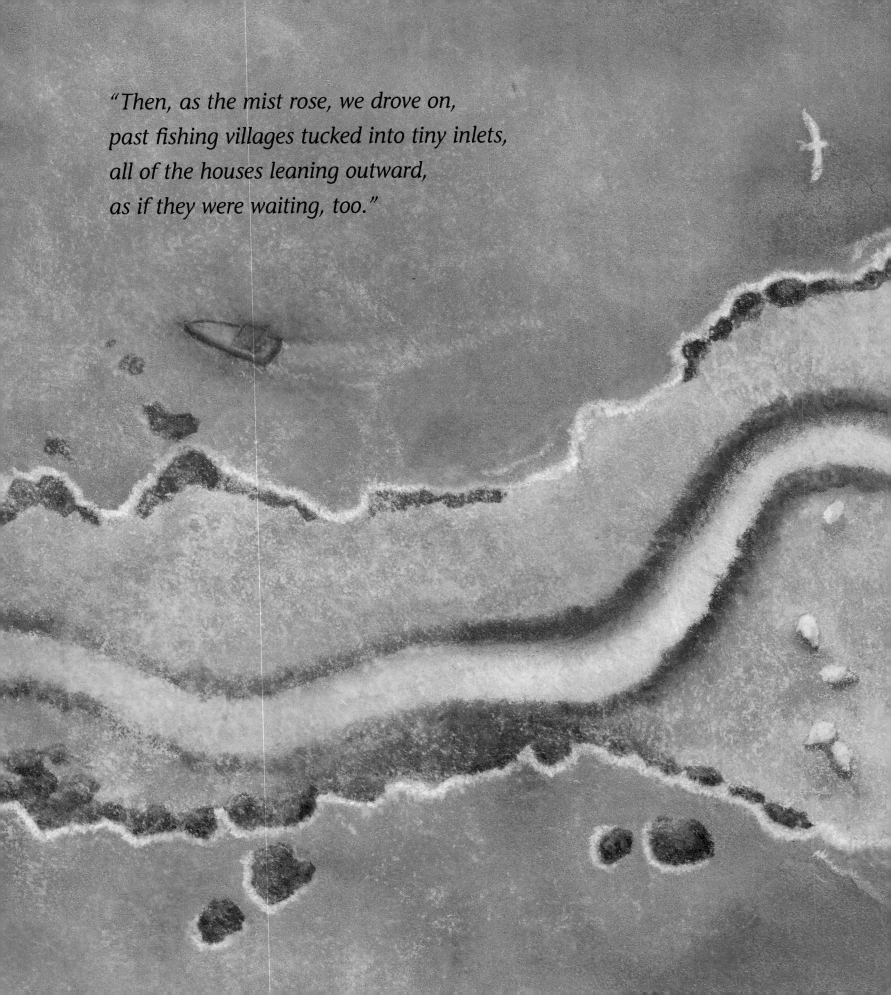

"Then, as the mist rose, we drove on,
past fishing villages tucked into tiny inlets,
all of the houses leaning outward,
as if they were waiting, too."

"'Is this the day?' I wondered.
'Is this the one?'

Gulls followed us, wheeling and calling,
diving into the wind as if it were water."

"I couldn't wait any longer,
so we stopped the car and
I called the hospital again."

"Was it the day?" asked Jamie.
"The day I was born?"
Aunt Isabel smiled.

"This time, finally, they put
your mom on the phone.
'Well,' your mom said, 'he's here.
And we're just getting to know each other.'"

"'Yippee!' I called out to your uncle.
'He's here!'"

"That was me?" Jamie yawned.
"It was," Aunt Isabel nodded.
"Then what happened?" Jamie asked.

"And then," Aunt Isabel said,
"since we wouldn't get to see you
until the next day,
we drove to the edge of the land,
to the lighthouse that waits there,
guiding the ships in from the sea."

"We danced in the waves that broke on the shore,
and we sang out our greeting to you,
with seagulls turning and spinning overhead
and the water swirling and splashing around our feet."

"'Welcome to this day,' we sang.
'Your very first one.'"

"You did that?" Jamie asked.
Aunt Isabel hugged Jamie tight.

"Yes," she whispered.
*"We sat with the evening until it turned into night,
until the moon rose over us
and we fell asleep, dreaming of you,
shining too,
a new soul in this world."*

All of a sudden, the phone rang.
Aunt Isabel handed it to Jamie,
and Jamie heard his daddy and mommy say,
"Well, she's here! Your new baby sister.
And we're just getting to know each other."
"Yippee!" Jamie cheered. "She's here!"

And then, because they wouldn't get to
see her until the next day,
Aunt Isabel and Jamie
sat among the cats and the bedcovers
and sang out their greeting to her.

"Welcome to this day!" they sang.
"Your very first one.
Welcome."

And then they turned out all the lights,
all over the house,
except for one—

Jamie's nightlight shaped like a seashell,
shining just for her,
for Jamie's brand-new baby sister.